A PARIS-CHIEN ADVENTURE

HUDSON *in* PROVENCE

JACKIE CLARK MANCUSO

LA LIBRAIRIE PARISIENNE

OTHER BOOKS IN THE SERIES

Paris-Chien: Adventures of an Expat Dog

Library of Congress Cataloging-in-Publication Data
Mancuso, Jackie Clark, author, illustrator.
Hudson in Provence : a Paris-chien adventure / Jackie Clark Mancuso.
pages cm
Summary: "Hudson, an American dog living in Paris, goes on vacation to Provence, where he plunges into the lives of the working provençal dogs he meets, and discovers a talent he didn't know he had."
ISBN 978-0-9886058-4-8 (hardcover)
[1. Dogs--Fiction. 2. Provence-Côte d'Azur (France)--Fiction. 3. France--Fiction.] I. Title.
PZ7.1.M364Hu 2015
[E]--dc23
2014041968

Printed in China. This product conforms to CPSIA 2008.

ISBN 978-0-9886058-4-8

10 9 8 7 6 5 4 3 2

For Hudson and Steve.
I couldn't have done it without you.

There's music that
announces train
arrivals and departures
TGV
SNCF

Hi, I'm Hudson.

It's August in Paris. That means it's vacation time!

My mom and I are taking the super fast *TGV* train to Provence, in the south of France.

We're staying in an old stone
house in the middle of a vineyard.

Provence is a magical place.
My book says artists come here
to paint because it's so beautiful.

And the *provençal* dogs work.

I want to do what they do,
so I can feel the magic.

I don't want to just be a tourist.
I want to be a *provençal* dog.

la lune

la chaise

PROVENCE
THE MAGIC of PROVENCE
le lit

Today we're at the beach
on the *Côte d'Azur*.
My mom is swimming
and I'm chasing seagulls.

It's the prettiest beach
I've ever seen.

les mouettes
maman

It's evening at the *place*.
There are dogs everywhere!

Cafe du Centre

"*Bonjour, je m'appelle* Hudson.
I'm visiting from Paris.
I read that dogs work here."

"Wow! I want to do that.
Will you show me how?"

"*Salut*, I'm Gaston.

Yes, we're working dogs.
I'm a border collie. I herd sheep."

"You really want to learn?
Okay. I'll show you."

"Sometimes the sheep wander off.
My job is to keep them together.

I stare at them to show
I'm in charge. Then I herd
them to the pasture."

les moutons

When I try it, they just stare back,
like THEY want to herd ME.

l'arbre

Qui est ce petit bonhomme?

Gaston says *"c'est évident"*
I don't have a herding instinct.

He introduced me to Philippe.
It's not every day you meet
a truffle hunter!

"Truffles are smelly mushrooms
that grow underground near
trees. They're delicious!
I have been specially trained
to sniff them out because
people like them too."

"Could you show me how?
I want to do everything
provençal dogs do."

I sniffed and dug
under one tree...no luck.

...then another.

ma maison

Where are those tasty truffles?

Hudson, stop digging up the yard! Come watch the *Tour de France* with me.

le vélo

The most famous bicycle race in the world is coming through our town.

I don't want to watch. I want to ride!

Yikes! They go fast.

Am I seeing things or is that a dog riding behind us?

"Huddie, are you feeling the magic of Provence?"

"Well...it's beautiful here, but..."

"But what?"

"The sheep didn't pay attention when I tried to herd them, I couldn't find a truffle for you, and the cyclists went so fast I couldn't keep up. I'm not good at *provençal* things."

"You think the magic is going to come from doing what everybody else is doing.

What if it comes from doing something *you* want to do?"

maman
I have the BEST mom!

My mom gave me a painting set!

Now I'm painting the landscape
en plein air just like the great artists
Cezanne, Matisse, de Staël,
and Van Gogh.

I like painting!

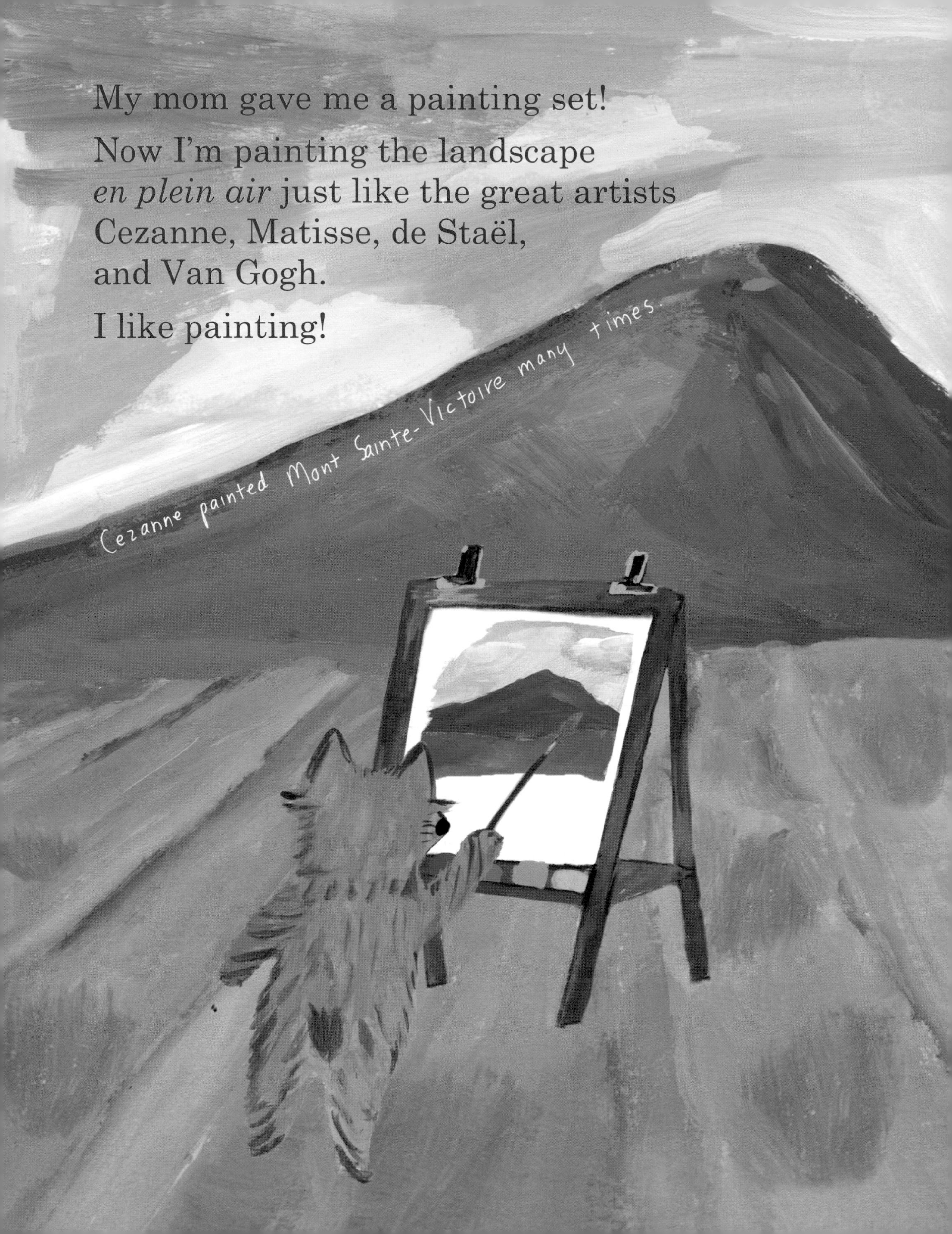

And I know why they liked to paint outdoors...

...because it smells so good!

I also like painting in the *Place*.
It's a good way to meet other dogs.

PLAT
Entrée
playing boules

GLACES
BANANE
CAFÉ
CAPUCCINO
CARAMEL BEURRE SALLÉ
CHOCOLAT
FLEUR DE LAIT
JASMINE
LAVANDE
M+Ms
NOISETTE
NOIX
PISTACHE
ROSE
VANILLE
VIOLETTE
SORBETS
ABRICOT
ANANAS
CASSIS
CITRON
FRAISE
FRAMBOISE
MANGUE
MELON
MURE
ORANGE
PECHE
POIRE

Moi, j'adore la Pistache!

"Bonjour Sophie.
Who's your friend?"

"Bonjour Monsieur Glacier.
Hudson's visiting from Paris.
He's going to paint my portrait."

CLUB des
QUATRE PATTES

"Moi aussi."

I hope
he captures
my beautiful eyes.

“I’m next!”
“Will you paint me too?”

I'm so busy painting that the month flies by.

Now it's time to go home to Paris.

One month later in Provence...

"*Oh là là*. We got a postcard from Paris!"

la magie de Provence
exposition d'un nouveau peintre
Shows promise, for a dog.
"At first it was pure instinct... technique came later."
It's like having my Provence friends with me in Paris!

I could do that!

Some people think it's funny that a dog paints. I don't. I think some of the magic of Provence rubbed off on me.